THE SMURF CHAMPIONSHIP GAMES

by Peyo

Ready-to-Read

Simon Spotlight

New York   London   Toronto   Sydney   New Delhi

SIMON SPOTLIGHT

An imprint of Simon & Schuster Children's Publishing Division

1230 Avenue of the Americas, New York, New York 10020

For information about special discounts for bulk purchases, please contact

Simon & Schuster Special Sales at 1-866-506-1949 or business@simonandschuster.com.

Manufactured in the United States of America 0612 LAK

First Edition

2 4 6 8 10 9 7 5 3 1

ISBN 978-1-4424-4993-0 (pbk)

ISBN 978-1-4424-4994-7 (hc)

It was a quiet morning in Smurf Village.
The only sound was a rooster crowing.
All the Smurfs were asleep.
Smurfs don't like to get up early!

There was one Smurf who was awake.
Hefty Smurf had been exercising
since the sun came up.

Hefty is good at track, swimming, jumping—everything!
But he still felt sad.
That afternoon, Papa Smurf asked Hefty what was wrong.

"Why should I bother training, Papa?" Hefty asked. "I always come in first place. But I always come in last place, too! There is no one to compete against."

Papa and Hefty walked through
the village.
All the Smurfs were relaxing.
Some played chess. Some fished.
Some played darts.
No one wanted to exercise!

"We should do something to get everyone excited about exercising," said Papa. "How about the Smurf Championship Games?"

Hefty loved Papa's idea, so
the very next day he made
an announcement.
"Come sign up for the first Smurf
Championship Games," he said.
"The winner will receive a medal."

"Medals don't smurf much to me,"
said a Smurf.
"And I will give the winner a kiss,"
Smurfette said.
All the Smurfs rushed to sign up!

Now everyone wanted to play!
There were so many Smurfs,
Papa told them they needed to
divide into two teams.
"I would like to play too!" Weakling
Smurf said.

No one wanted Weakling on their team.
"Sorry. We're full," said the red team.
"Sorry. We're all full too," said
the yellow team.

Weakling started to walk away,
but Hefty stopped him.
"If you want to play, no one can
stop you from smurfing in the
games on your own," Hefty said.
"Great," said Weakling. "I hope I
win first place!"

The next day was the first day
of practice.
All the Smurfs had to get up early.

Nobody felt like exercising
except for Weakling Smurf.
He arrived early and
started running drills.

But in the middle of a race, he collapsed, completely exhausted. All the other Smurfs laughed.

"Don't smurf any attention
to them," Hefty said.
"Keep practicing and
you'll be fine!"
But as the day went on, Weakling
learned that he wasn't very good at
any of the sports.

At the hammer throw, he dropped
the hammer right on Hefty's foot.

He was terrible at gymnastics, too.
And all the other Smurfs kept laughing.

Weakling went to talk to Papa Smurf.
"Are you ready for the games?"
Papa asked.
Weakling said sadly, "No, Papa. I've
decided not to play."

Papa didn't want Weakling to
give up.
He had an idea.

Papa gave Weakling a small pot
filled with thick, red liquid.
"Before each game, smurf this
cream on your nose," Papa said.
"It will help you win.
But don't tell anyone!"
That night, Weakling dreamed he
was a champion!

The day of the big games arrived!
The first game was a relay race.
Weakling put a little magic cream
on his nose.
The members of each team had
to take turns running, then pass a
baton to the next player.

Both teams cheated.
The red team dipped
the yellow team's baton in glue.
And the yellow team covered
the red team's baton in soap!

The yellow team's runner could not
let go of his baton,
and the red team's runner could
not hold on to the baton.
But Weakling only had to pass the
baton to himself, from one hand to
the other.
Weakling won the race!

Weakling played like a champion.
When it was time for the high jump,
he cleared the bar. Everyone was
shocked, except for Papa.

The Smurfs began cheering for Weakling. Weakling came in first in every event!

The last event of the day was the marathon. Weakling was determined to win.

As the race wore on, Weakling felt tired.

He put more magic cream on his nose. But as he approached the finish line, his legs began to shake. Weakling decided to quit.

He stopped on the side of the road. But Weakling didn't see the thorns on the bushes.

They stung him so badly he began to run faster than he ever did before. Weakling zoomed past everyone in the race and took first place!

The Smurfs carried Weakling to
the platform.
It was time to give him the gold
medal.
But Weakling had to stop them.
"No!" he cried. "I can't accept it.
I cheated. I used a magic cream
that Papa smurfed for me."

"You didn't do that, did you, Papa?"
Hefty asked.
Papa Smurf smiled. "It's true that I
gave him something:
strawberry jelly!"

"You felt stronger because you believed the cream was magic," Papa explained. "Weakling, you don't owe your victory to anyone but yourself. You deserve to smurf this medal." Everyone cheered for Weakling Smurf, the champion of the Smurf Championship Games!